THE BEAST OF BASQUE

Tales of the Ravensdaughter - Adventure One

Erin Hunt Rado

The characters and events portrayed in this book are fictitious. Any similarity to real persons, living or dead, is coincidental and not intended by the author.

ISBN-13: 9798839531079

Cover design by: Erin Hunt Rado
Printed in the United States of America

Thanks, Kitty, for the name
And as always for my beloved Paul.

Also, I would like to acknowledge Christopher Fain for listening to all those late-night ideas.

AUTHOR'S NOTE

Tales of the Ravensdaughter is a six-part epic fantasy novella series that begins with the heroine reacting to a recent assault. I mention this because readers who are survivors have asked me to caveat the opening in some way.

However, the first story, and indeed the entire series, is about reclaiming one's power. In *The Beast of Basque*, Alerice Linden does endure trauma, but then she embarks upon a life she could never have imagined. By forgiving that trauma - though never forgetting it - she discovers a power she is ready and willing to wield. When Alerice encounters other victims, she acts to save them. In so doing, she comes to terms with her trauma, and refuses to allow it to define her.

I hope my readers will find this acceptable. And now I invite you to read *The Beast of Basque*, Adventure One from *Tales of the Ravensdaughter*.

When the Serpent Father Fire
Loves the Mother Water Wind,
When L'Orku's breath of thunder
'Cross the mighty sky ascends;

When wings of ravens black
Stir shadows in the mist,
The Realme may kiss Mortalia
And a new child will be blessed.

- from the Scrolls of Imari

Alerice watched the revelers stuffing their faces. They were of little concern. Her target was the evening's host, Gotthard, mayor of Navre. She could still smell his scent on her skin. She could still hear his taunt after he had assaulted her and murdered her cousin. "Fly away, little bird, or this lion will catch you."

Alerice could not bear the echo of his disdain. Needing to think of something else, she focused on Gotthard's wife. The bejeweled sow sat guzzling beside her husband. Had she been the reason for Gotthard's attack? Had she been encouraging him to assert wanton dominance over every person in the city?

No, Gotthard was Gotthard. Untouchable by law, he was assured of his own righteousness, and he deserved the cup that Alerice had just placed before him.

She hid at the side of the feast hall dressed as a serving page. Candle sconces on the walls and candelabras on the tables could only illuminate so much, and there were more than enough shadows to conceal her. Shadows had always been her allies, and secluded within them Alerice took the measure of her mark.

Gotthard entertained Lord Andoni, the Prime Cheval of Navre, and with good reason. The Cheval had appointed Gotthard as mayor, which had given him license to go wherever he pleased and take whatever he fancied.

Three nights ago, he had fancied Alerice after a chance encounter had gone terribly wrong. A furious Gotthard had been leading some of the constabulary to round up his drunken notary. Alerice had been trying to pry the notary away from his cup, but when Gotthard had seen her, he decided to show the notary how innocent people would pay for his staff's errant behavior.

Alerice's fists clenched as Gotthard and Andoni engaged in jovial chitchat. Time was of the essence if she was going to escape. Serving pages were already gathering in the hallway. If she could make it past them and out the kitchen's back door, the shadowed streets outside would conceal her.

If Gotthard would just drink his damned cup.

Gotthard rose to toast his guest, as did the assembly.

"Friends," he began, flashing a grin that far too many people found charismatic.

Alerice tensed, for the up-twist of Gotthard's lips caused the memory of that expression to flash across her eyes. She had seen it when he had forced her down over a bar table, cast her skirts up over her back, and taken her from behind. The fabric had felt like a shroud. She had locked her jaw, for she had refused to give Gotthard the satisfaction of hearing her cry out. However, she had managed to look back at the beast.

Just in time to see him kill Cousin Jerome! Jerome protected the tavern. He had tried to stop the assault, and what had Gotthard done? He had ordered the constabulary men to take hold of him and force him to watch. Then Gotthard had ordered one of them to stab Jerome as Gotthard finished with Alerice, grabbed her scalp, and cast her aside.

Thinking of Jerome brought tears, which Alerice desperately fought back. She turned and pressed her brow into the wall to prevent a rush of anguish. For these past three nights, she had been completely numb, unable to feel a single thing, pleasurable or painful. Now she suddenly felt everything – and now was not the time.

But poor Jerome. Poor Cousin Millie, Jerome's wife, who worked in Gotthard's kitchen and had helped her gain entry a moment ago. Poor Uncle Judd, Aunt Carol, Grammy Linden, and Jerome's three brothers who were no doubt spoiling for revenge. Gotthard had ruined an entire family in one heinous moment, and then he had proclaimed Alerice guilty of Jerome's murder to exonerate himself and prevent her from seeking refuge with those she loved.

"Sukaar, Father Fire," Alerice silently prayed. *"Imari, Mother Water Wind. Give me strength in this moment."*

Alerice felt her emotions drain away, and she turned back to her task. She wanted to shove a dagger into Gotthard's heart, but she could not get close enough to stab him and flee.

It was best to let the cup do its work, but she would make herself known. Partly to call Gotthard out, but mostly to show everyone that a small person was capable of standing up. Her father had always taught her to stand up when she could make a difference. Now she meant to.

"For the Cheval is indeed a noble man, and we praise him for his good graces," Gotthard said. "To the Cheval."

"To the Cheval," all assembled repeated.

Alerice drew out a small knife as the revelers drank. Gotthard took one swallow and another, but then stopped mid-draught. He rankled his nose and glanced at the cup, which he handed to his wife, who eagerly drained it dry.

Did he drink enough? Was this going to work?

The only sound Alerice could hear was her own heartbeat. The only sensation she could feel was her quickening breath.

Gotthard licked his lips while offering Andoni a smug little bow. Andoni responded by standing and extending his arm in brotherly friendship. Gotthard took it in a hand-to-forearm grasp. Then he began thinly smacking his lips.

A sudden *bleetch* erupted at the head table as Gotthard's wife vomited up the bloody contents of her stomach. All turned to her aghast and Alerice prayed that Gotthard would likewise splay his innards.

His wife moaned and vomited again. The Reef of Navre leaped up from his seat at a lower table and hurried to help her.

Then Gotthard doubled over, clutching his gut. He reached for the Reef and caught hold of his tunic, but he too vomited over the dinner and flatware, his blood and bits of food mixing with those of his wife.

Gotthard hoisted himself upright despite his obvious pain, and Alerice launched the blade at him. It sank into his shoulder, attracting all eyes.

She stood out from the shadows and tore away her page cap. Her blonde hair tumbled down past her shoulders as she summoned the full measure of the rage that was deservedly hers.

"There's a peck from this little bird! Mayor Gotthard murdered my cousin, Jerome Linden!"

"Take her!" the Reef shouted, gesturing for his men to advance from the hall's corners.

Alerice turned and bolted down the hall. She hurled herself at the pages, scattering their dessert trays. She heard the clatter of metal on stone as she sprinted into the kitchen.

She made for a table filled with pots awaiting washing, and knocked them all to the floor. The head cook stood bolt upright and the rest of the staff watched in shock, allowing Alerice to shoot for the back door.

One of the Reef's men entered and called for someone to shut the door. Alerice saw Cousin Millie respond, which was a ploy to keep the Reef from suspecting her. Alerice grabbed the copper pan that Millie had placed on a nearby stool and smacked her across the jaw with it to send her toppling backward.

Then she hurried out into the night's blessed shadows.

***

Alerice knew every nook and cranny in Navre. She had come to the city at the age of five. Uncle Judd had taken her in at her mother's request after her father had died in Lord Andoni's ranks, serving honorably during the campaign against southern invaders.

Uncle Judd had praised Alerice for her quick wit and natural charm. He had doted on her as his own daughter, likely because he had been blessed with four boys and needed an angel to brighten his day.

Alerice had eagerly learned to manage a household, but while she was an adequate cook and seamstress, sophisticated chores had been her delight.

Uncle Judd owned the local brewery, and Alerice soon began taking stock of how much grain arrived each day, how much water the brewery drew from the nearby river, and how many barrels were properly ripened. She had been quick to learn ledgers and tallies, and how to make certain that inventory went unpilfered.

When Alerice had reached the age when most girls would have been sold in marriage, Uncle Judd could not bear to part with her. Instead, he had cooked up a scheme with Grammy Linden to marry her to Cousin Jerome, all the while placing them both at the new tavern that Judd had acquired in a card game.

Alerice had always wondered if Uncle Judd had cheated to win the establishment, which he renamed the Cup and Quill. While he had never spoken of the matter, she had been happy to learn the inn-keeping trade.

There had been so many things to manage – larder stocks, meats and cheeses, breads and treats. And the girls. They kept rooms upstairs and sold their company during the evening hours. Even though Mistress Dora kept track of each 'busy lassie', Alerice had seen to the tidiness of their lodgings and knew she would manage the girls herself one day.

And that day had come when Uncle Judd had placed her in charge of the Cup and Quill. She and Jerome had shared a quick cousins' kiss to end their engagement, which everyone knew had been little more than a sweet deception. Jerome had married Millie shortly thereafter while Alerice had 'taken the apron'.

Folk had likened it to taking holy vows. As the new mistress of the Cup and Quill, Alerice had plied each of Uncle Judd's management lessons with firm precision. Cousin Jerome helped as best he could, although he had doted upon Millie as any newlywed husband should. Even so, Alerice had been able to balance his married life with her independent one to make the Cup and Quill one of the most popular public houses in Navre.

Until the three nights before when Gotthard had

shattered her world and sent her hiding in the city's backstreets, where she had been forced to slip silently to and fro, stealing food wherever she could find it and huddling for warmth whenever a hovel presented itself.

After the attack, Alerice had waited for the moment when she could steal back to the brewery without attracting attention. She would stop only to bid her family farewell, for lingering would implicate them in Gotthard's trumped-up charges regarding Jerome.

Yet as Alerice had waited, she had crawled behind the apothecary. The rear door's inner bolt had been secure, but not the side window's. Fortunately, Uncle Judd had insisted that she learn to read more than ledgers. She held a basic understanding of tinctures and medicines, and thus she had been able to identify the ingredients necessary to mix a swift-acting poison as the trauma of what Gotthard had done had begun to take hold of her exhausted wits.

In that instant, she had formed a new plan, one she could execute as Gotthard hosted Lord Andoni.

***

Alerice cast a weary gaze upward at her new traveling companions, three circling ravens that cawed into the night sky. She plodded down the open road on the bare back of a stolen plow horse. She wore stolen clothes, and a stolen pack containing stolen food rested across her shoulders. She was a thief. She was a murderess, and she was... alone.

She would never see her family again. She would never be able to curl into Uncle Judd's arms or have Grammy Linden sing her to sleep. She had never had the opportunity to say goodbye to any of them. After killing Gotthard, she did not dare go anywhere near the brewery.

Had standing up to that beast been worth it? Gotthard had taken everything from her – her dignity, her livelihood, and her self-respect. The last was the worst, for now that all was done, Alerice could not justify killing him. She certainly could not justify killing his wife. Indeed, who was she to have taken such action in the first place?

The ravens cawed again in low, throaty tones. More joined them until there were at least a dozen. They might as well have been vultures. Alerice was already dead in her own eyes. She could never use her own name again. She could never confide in another person again.

Had this all truly happened in a few scant days?

The horse clip-clopped on down the treeless road. More caws sounded and Alerice looked up a third time. Clouds shadowed the moon, creating a gray background for the ravens' flight. As they circled, her thoughts swirled.

Then she smiled, for she found herself back in her bedroom at the Cup and Quill. Somewhere in her oh-so-sleepy mind, she was aware that the plow horse had stopped moving and stood quietly in the open, but she paid it no heed as she bent forward and nestled against a broad horsehair pillow.

Something *thunked* into Alerice's pack with enough force to jolt her forward. The plow horse startled and whinnied, and then hurried off as Alerice toppled from its back onto the roadside. She landed on her hip as her pack flew off of her shoulder, a crossbow bolt sticking out of it.

Another bolt *whizzed* in, landing a hand's width from her head, and Alerice looked up to see three mounted men galloping straight for her. There was no mistaking that the Reef of Navre rode in the lead position.

The clouds parted overhead and the moon seemed to spotlight her. Alerice's heart leaped and she ran, but there was no outpacing her pursuers. In moments, three horses surrounded her and three men jumped down to the grass, two with loaded crossbows trained on her, and the Reef fitting a fresh bolt into his.

Alerice froze and stared at him. The Reef leveled his bow and shot her in the shoulder. The impact knocked her to her haunches, and she cried out in pain.

"That's for pecking the mayor, little bird."

The other two men laughed as the Reef said to them, "What do you know, Tom? You did see someone ride away on old Pat's plow nag. Guess we'll have to wrangle it up and return it to him."

"Guess so," Tom said. "Funny how the ravens led us straight to her."

The Reef looked up at the dispersing flock. "Yes, funny." He paused to listen to the receding caws before he looked down at Alerice. "The gods below must really want this one."

Rage and fear welled up within Alerice as the Reef stepped close. She drew her dagger from her belt and crouched to spring up at him, but he rushed forward and dropped to a knee beside her, tossing his crossbow down so that he could place his gloved hand over hers and control her blade. Then he grabbed her by the hair and wrenched her head back.

The intimacy was terrifying. Alerice tried to summon the courage to fight, but she had no hope in besting him – and she was well aware, that he was well aware, of this fact.

She scratched at his face with her free hand, but Tom advanced to take hold of her arm. She struggled and kicked, but the third man came forward to step hard on one of her thighs. The Reef adjusted his position to kneel on the other.

"I should take you back to Navre," he said, looking her over with the confidence of a hunter watching an animal struggle in a steel trap. "I should hang you for what you did to Gotthard and his wife, but I think I will kill you here instead. I'll let the wolves take your flesh, and whoever wants you below take your soul. And that will be the sad end of tiny, little you."

He forced Alerice's hand toward her body and

pricked the dagger into her ribs. She did not cry out, for the shoulder pain numbed her to the cut. Instead, she locked stares with him and breathed hard through her nose.

"You see," the Reef continued. "If I hang you, your family will have the right to claim your body. They will bury you at their brewery, and take solace knowing what happened to you. Instead, I will take this knife of yours, and leave it on their doorstep, and let them wonder. They'll know it's yours, won't they?"

Alerice could not deny that they would.

"Of course, I could arrest them all as your accomplices," the Reef added. "But why would I ruin Navre's beer supply?"

The men agreed, and Alerice's eyes narrowed as she struggled one final time to free herself. The one man pressed harder on her thigh, and she grunted in pain. Alerice glanced up at him, and then leveled her stare at the Reef and spat in his face.

He did not seem to mind. "Now, that's a kiss goodbye."

The Reef drew close. His beard stubble scratched Alerice's skin, and she thought he was going to force his lips onto hers, but he exhaled on her cheek as he wrenched the dagger from her grasp.

"And by the way, thank you," the Reef said softly. "With Gotthard gone, I am free to rise."

The Reef shoved the dagger into Alerice's ribcage. She screamed at the searing pain, and her body tensed as the steel pierced deeply. Somehow, she felt the dagger's tip touch her heart, but then she felt nothing further.

***

Something poked Alerice's shoulder. It poked a second time and then a third, each time deeper than the last. Alerice tried to wave it off, but she could not lift her arm. She was able to move her shoulder ever so slightly, but nothing more.

"What do you know?" someone said. "It lives, and it's awake."

What do you mean, it lives and it's awake?

Alerice tried to voice the thought, but all she could manage were a few thin moans. Was she waking from the nightmare that she longed to escape? Was it all finally over?

"Hello, mortal..." the same person said in a sing-song tone.

"Uhmph," Alerice groaned before she contracted her gut to force enough air through her chest to comment, "mortal?"

"Ah, would you listen to that. It also talks."

"Unh. Of course... I talk." Alerice thought she should punctuate her statement with something equal to the present sarcasm, but her thoughts swirled too greatly to summon a retort.

"Come, come, little flesh pot. Let's wake up all the way. They're waiting to see you."

Alerice sighed internally. None of this made any

sense. However, the one thing she could comprehend was that the someone engaging her was going to keep doing so until she rose from her slumber, for that's what her present state must be. A slumber the likes of which she had never known.

The someone addressing her began tapping on her forehead, which was the most exacerbating sensation thus far, and Alerice finally found the strength to heft her arm and flail her hand about her brow to bat the someone away. Then, slowly, she opened her eyes.

A spry youth came into her line of sight. He hovered over her, his ice-blue eyes dancing. His whitish hair seemed alive with tiny sparks of different colors. His lips were deep peach, and he grinned with curiosity before he reached out to tap Alerice's brow once again.

"Please stop that," she said, moving her head away.

"Oh!" the youth exclaimed as he raised an eyebrow and inspected Alerice more closely. "It has manners."

"And please stop calling me 'it'." She drew in a deep breath as she began to feel more stable, and blinked widely a few times before she focused on the youth again. "My name is Alerice Linden. Of Navre."

"Well, that's interesting. Not that I either know where Navre is, or care for that matter, but Alerice... I do like that name. It's pretty, and I suppose it suits you because, for a mortal, you're somewhat pretty yourself."

"Why do you keep calling me 'mortal'?" she asked.

"Well, you're hardly anything else. Now, Alerice Linden of Navre, can you sit up?"

"I... think so, but I'm having trouble moving. I've never felt like this before."

"Oh, that's not surprising. You've never been dead before."

"What?"

"Ah, I didn't realize that you were hard of hearing. I can speak louder if it helps!" the youth shouted.

"No, I can hear everything you say, but did you just say I was dead?"

"Yes, and I must admit that's puzzling. Normally, mortals leave their bodies above while their souls come to us. But you came in as a complete package, didn't you. You even had a crossbow bolt stuck in your shoulder, but I took that out. You're welcome, by the way. Now, once more. Can you sit up? I'll help you if you like."

"Thank you," Alerice said softly.

"My pleasure," the youth said in a slightly higher, more feminine register. Alerice focused on rising as he reached down and lifted her torso away from her body so that she sat up within the shell of herself.

She looked down at her legs and then around and over her shoulder at her torso and head. Her body lay peacefully with her arms at her sides, still dressed in the clothes she had stolen.

Alerice blinked, dumbfounded, but then as she looked back at the youth, she startled in alarm. He had become a maiden with soft rose lips and waist-long whitish hair shimmering with colors along its length.

"What... are you?" Alerice gasped.

"You mean, who am I?" the maiden asked.

"No, I mean 'what' are you? Are you spirit? For I fear that you are not flesh."

"Yes, you do have that part right. My name is Oddwyn, Herald to the King of Shadows and the Raven Queen."

"Shadows? Ravens?" Alerice said to herself. "Then that means..."

A quick flash of her final moments with the Reef shot across her mind's eye, and Alerice found herself reliving the strike of her own dagger into her heart.

"Ohhh, there's that little memory angst you mortals do," Oddwyn cooed in a voice as sweet as any loving sister's. "It gets me every time. Since you're a bit overwhelmed right now, I'll try to explain things. You are in the Realme, both your spirit and your body, and again this is quite puzzling. That's why the king and queen want to see you."

"In the Realme?" Alerice asked.

"Yes," Oddwyn said, again presenting himself as a youth. "The Evherealme. This is the Convergence."

Alerice looked about, finding four towering filigree arches crafted of shimmering silver-veined stone. Each bore glyphs the likes of which she had never seen. They were set at quarter opposites to one another, and four smaller arches rested between each to form a wondrous octagon. A filigree stone copula rose high above, supported by the arches. Its apex seemed to extend toward infinity.

An ether of black, midnight blue, and deep teal pulsed within each arch, and Alerice could see the same ether wisping about the copula's filigree.

Then the ether in several arches began to swirl, and people floated through. They appeared thin and ethereal, some old, some young, and even a few abandoned babes. The moment they entered, pale spirits came to meet them, taking their hands and guiding them a few paces before they all vanished.

Alerice startled again, for the Convergence was both beautiful and demoralizing. She felt her heart sink as she turned her face aside to hide a sensation of utter loss.

"Now, what's all this?" Oddwyn asked, gently reaching out to take Alerice's chin and turn her face back. "Don't cry. As I said, you are very interesting."

"Please just leave me be," Alerice said as she saw more souls entering through the Convergence arch near her, only to be led away by more pale spirits.

"Now, now. The Realme's master and mistress are waiting to see you. You should feel honored to have the chance to speak to them."

"Should I?" Alerice said, finally finding enough strength to encase her loss in sarcasm. "You said your name was Oddwyn? Would that be short for 'odd one'? The name certainly suits you if this is so."

"Hmmm. And I thought you had manners. Well,

if this is how you wish to converse, then let's be flat about it. First, being odd is a perfectly wonderful state of self. I would rather be odd than be anything else, and anyone who does not see the truth in that statement is... what's the phrase I'm looking for... oh yes – a dead mortal."

Oddwyn gestured his thumb at more souls entering the Convergence through other arches.

"Like them. Dead, dead, and dead. Second," he said with a hard flick on her brow. "Accept your situation and get up. Leave your body where it lies. It's not going anywhere. You're coming with me." Oddwyn held up his fingers to snap, even as the tri-colored ether in the arch behind Alerice began to swirl. "Now."

***

Alerice found herself standing in a space that seemed both vast and intimate. It bore no architectural definitions, but it was definitely a 'place'. She had no idea how she had traveled here. She suspected it had been through the Convergence arch, but as she glanced about to find it, she discovered the youthful Oddwyn standing beside her.

He wore an iridescent tunic of turquoise and lavender, accented by indigo and pearl. His shirt was crafted from some shimmering ethereal material, and his light-blue trousers tucked into white boots.

Oddwyn flashed a 'what are you looking at?'

expression before he gestured that Alerice should look ahead.

Though she had not seen anything a moment ago, Alerice now beheld two otherworldly figures standing atop a dais.

Oddwyn stepped forward and bowed to them both. Then he turned toward Alerice and proclaimed, "Mortal, lower your gaze in awe. Bend your knee in respect, for I present to you the King of Shadows and the Raven Queen, master and mistress of the Evherealme."

Alerice stared wide-eyed at Oddwyn, half-paralyzed in fear and completely uncertain of what to do. Oddwyn gestured that she should look down, which Alerice did while offering a small curtsey. Then, she glanced back up at Oddwyn, who half-rolled his eyes at her meager gesture and returned to her side.

Alerice looked up at the two majesties, and her breath came up short, for she recognized what Grammy Linden had often described as the King of Shadows and his wife, the Raven Queen.

No stories of allegorical lore told to children by the fireside could have prepared Alerice for this moment.

The king was tall. The tone of his long, open robe shifted as though affected by the movement of light. His face was long and pale. His eyes were dark gray and he sported a thin beard trimmed close to his jawline. His crown was crafted of shimmering smokey crystals. Longer crystals adorned his pauldrons while an intricate crystalline trim ran along the border of his robe's vertical opening, its hem, and its cuffs. The king's physical form hidden, within his robe, seemed to shift, as anyone might expect of a shadow.

The Raven Queen stood in a gown of sleek feathers that fluxed from black to purple to emerald. Her arms were white as willows. Her crown was crafted of a silverish metal Alerice had never seen, even for an inn mistress well experienced in coin. Her black hair flowed nearly to her feet, billowing as if buoyed by unseen currents. Her eyes were the deepest amethyst, and her lips the deepest red.

Behind the king stood two Shadow Warriors.

Behind the queen stood two Raven Knights.

The Shadow Warriors' breastplates were etched with wispy curls about the articulations. The same curls adorned their arm and leg plates, but what unnerved Alerice was the lack of faces within their helms. She could only see gray-blackness therein.

The Raven Knights' helms were metal bird skulls. Golden orbs shone through the eye sockets. Sprays of metal feathers rose up from the top-back of the helms' crestlines. The edges of the layered plates along their arms and legs were fashioned to resemble metal feather tips, and Alerice could not be certain if their long, black, feather-trimmed cloaks weren't wings.

Oddwyn drew a breath and proclaimed, "Your

Majesties, I present to you Alerice Linden of Navre."

Not having the slightest idea what more was expected, Alerice curtseyed again.

The King of Shadows and the Raven Queen nodded in response. "You are welcome to the Hall of Eternity," they said, their voices at an octave from one another.

Alerice shivered and reached out to take Oddwyn's hand. Oddwyn looked at the gesture, then at Alerice. Then Oddwyn became a maiden once again, her tunic transforming into a lady's belted demi-gown with sleeves that extended over the tops of her fingers and a length which displayed her light-blue leggings and white boots. She gave Alerice's hand a reassuring squeeze.

The king gestured to his right while the queen gestured to her left. In response, the hall took on the semblance of a columned rotunda with shimmering statues of male warriors along the king's hemisphere and women of the arts along the queen's.

Great glyphs appeared about the floor, giving it a mosaic quality. Thrones appeared upon the dais, the king's crafted with bunched spears along the sides, and the queen's crafted with raven heads looking out at side angles. Their dazzling golden eyes matched those of her Raven Knights.

The king and queen sat in a unified motion, the Shadow Warriors and Raven Knights advancing behind them. Then they bade Alerice to step forward.

Alerice gave Oddwyn's hand one final squeeze,

prayed that the gods above would somehow protect her, and stepped toward the dais. She was shaking. She could not help it, but no matter how terrified she was, she made up her mind to endure the moment.

"Set your fear aside," the queen said in a dark honey voice.

"No," said the king. "Wear your fear openly. Show it for all to see. Only by exposing it shall you master it."

"Yes, Your Majesty," Alerice forced herself to say. "But if you wish to see my fear, then may I ask, do I have reason to fear you? If I am dead, do you have further harm in store for me?"

Both the king and queen seemed pleasantly surprised by her response, as did Oddwyn, whom Alerice could not see but somehow sensed that he had presented himself as a youth again. She thought she heard him chuckle, but she remained fixed on the Realme's rulers, for whatever lay in store did so at their deciding.

The Raven Queen gestured her willow-white palm toward Alerice. As if touched by a comforting whisper, Alerice felt her heart strengthen and her shaking abate. She looked into the queen's amethyst eyes, suddenly feeling release from all mortal notions. In those eyes, she found the freedom of an unencumbered spirit, and along with it the joy of having known a life well lived.

"You are a good person, Alerice of Navre," the queen said. The king scoffed, but the queen paid him little heed. "At least, you have always tried to be good. I see this as I measure you."

Alerice wanted to accept the compliment. Grammy Linden would be pleased, for she had always cautioned the children in her care to live good lives. Grammy had always said that folks would be judged on their merits or faults one day. Knowing this, Alerice lowered her head, for her most egregious fault hung heavily over her.

"Forgive me, Your Majesty, but I am not good. I am a murderess, plain and simple."

Alerice felt the king taking pleasure from her admission, but she could also feel the queen pressing her amethyst gaze.

"You are damaged, Alerice," the queen said. "But before that damage, how did you live your life?"

"I always tried to stand up," Alerice replied, still unable to lift her head. "I never watered down the ale. I never cheated customers. I looked after the 'busy lassies', and I tried to host everyone at the Cup and Quill with equal measure. But I've killed two people, and I cannot escape that."

"And so you believe that one wrong choice discounts a life of good ones?"

Exactly why Alerice felt the courage to look upon the Raven Queen, she did not know, but she had considered this moral debate before, only now she was the culprit, not the inquisitor.

"Your Majesty, if a man steals to feed his family, he is still a thief. He may not be in the eyes of his neighbors, but he is in the eyes of those who rule. I took two lives, which is far worse than taking bread. I metered out justice. Who was I to do so?"

"A victim with no advocate," the queen stated. "There was no one to stand up for you. There was no one to stand up for other victims. You knew this as you plotted your course. You apportioned justice to a man who required it but would never have faced it, and if he had never injured you, you would have remained serving good ale and welcoming guests because, at heart, you are a good person."

"But I killed Gotthard's wife," Alerice said.

"Which was not your intent," the queen replied. "Your focus was on the wicked, as it should have been. There are folk above who applaud you for your actions, if you wish to know. What I wish to know is, if you had the power to hold the wicked accountable, would you wield it?"

Alerice had no reply. She had never thought of herself as judge and executioner, and she was not certain she wanted that responsibility. What if she made a mistake and judged the wrong person? What if she made things worse by killing someone wicked, but who had a good family?

"Your Majesty..." Alerice heard herself saying. "I have always tried to be good. Keeping faith with good deeds is something someone does when no one else bears witness, and it's always made sense to me. But I'm a modest person. Yes, I try to stand up when I can, but my father also cautioned me not to throw coins into other people's games. I am not the type to claim righteousness."

"But you could be," the king said. "If you were properly inspired. Look at you, girl. You have strength. Do you think you would be standing here without it?"

Alerice had no idea what to say, and as Grammy Linden had always cautioned, moments like these were the perfect time to say nothing.

The queen smiled.

"This one is mine," she said.

"Ah, let's see," the king replied.

"No," the queen asserted. "This one is mine. You had yours, My King, and we both know how well a driven man has served you. I will take this woman and her good deeds under my wing. I will help redeem her of the crime she accuses herself of committing, for her nature proffers true service."

"Indeed it does," the king said. "That's why I desire her."

The King of Shadows rose from his throne, and before Alerice could blink, he stood before her. He placed his hand upon her upper arm so that she could not back away and looked down at her.

"Alerice of Navre, I offer you power to defeat any enemy, either here in the Realme or above in Mortalia. You have the courage, and the will, to do this. I see it within you. You say you are modest, but I see pride, pride that you can use to your advantage. Take up my sword and swear your soul to me. You will never be a victim again, I promise you that."

"But My King," the queen said. "Another mortal already bears your blade. Do you intend to retrieve it from him?

The king did not reply as he pressed his dark-gray eyes into Alerice's soul.

Alerice felt icy tingles within her breast, and though they were not born of fear, she knew that she was not aligned with this immortal. And yet he had said...

"Mortalia, Your Majesty?"

The Raven Queen also appeared before Alerice and took hold of her other upper arm, though in a gentler manner.

"Mortalia is our term for the living world, and you are one of its unique souls. Sometimes, the gods above and we below intertwine. Sometimes our worlds kiss one another, and when such moments of divine currents flow together, mortal children are blessed with the gift to 'walk between'.

"That is why your whole self came unto the Convergence, your flesh and your spirit. That is why, if you swear to one of us, we can restore you to walk again among the living. But you will also be able to walk among the Realme's many worlds.

"If this notion appeals to you, swear yourself to me and I will give you my dagger to replace your own. With it, you may right wrongs done to others. You may stand up for those who have no voice, those who truly need you, and in so doing you may discover your own path to self-forgiveness."

Alerice looked between the king and queen, finding their desire to claim her distressing. Never in her life had she entered into an impulsive bargain. She had seen far too many of them at the Cup and Quill, and they rarely ended well. Now these immortals were asking for her to swear her soul?

"How can I possibly answer you?" Alerice said.

She regarded their hands, shrugged them off, and then backed away toward Oddwyn.

"You are telling me that I have some sort of special blessing? I don't believe in stories like that, and it's not likely I will start now. I don't know what to make of any of this, and now you both ask me to swear to you without knowing what this truly entails?"

She shook her head before she continued. "You could be asking me to do something dreadful. How am I to judge? Yes, Grammy Linden told me many stories of people who walk on after death, in the woods, or about the mountain tops, or along the seacoasts, but I have never heard tale of a spirit who roamed contentedly."

Alerice regarded the king, for he was correct in that she did have strength, perhaps even pride. "Forgive me, Your Majesty, but I have no enemies to defeat. This is because I've made none, and I do not wish to start. Even Gotthard was not my enemy. He was just a vile excuse for a man."

Then Alerice looked at the queen. "And while I sense that your manner is more appreciative of goodness, you are still the ruler of souls that can never see their families again, so how compassionate can you be?"

Alerice looked back and forth between them once more, then looked at their stalwart Shadow Warriors and Raven Knights, and then about the hall, where her eyes darted from face to face of the statues that seemed to be scrutinizing her.

"I... I just want to go home," she finally said, burying her face in her palms.

Alerice felt the Realme's master and mistress disappear from before her, and then she felt a gentle grip on both of her shoulders. She lifted her face to see the maiden Oddwyn looking at her with a supportive smile.

"They can, you know," Oddwyn said softly.

"They can what?" Alerice asked.

"The souls here can see their families. Some can even whisper to them and guide them. And you're special in that regard because you can do the same thing and still remain fully fleshed." Oddwyn resumed his youthful appearance to add, "Not that flesh is always a good thing."

Alerice smiled at Oddwyn's manner and his/her clear attempt at humor. "I'm sorry," she said.

"For what?" Oddwyn asked.

"For calling you 'odd' earlier. I shouldn't have done that."

"I've already told you that I prefer being odd."

"Yes, but I said it in a bad way. That was wrong. I

didn't mean to disparage you."

Oddwyn paused and then simply said, "Thank you." She resumed a maiden's form and brought Alerice into an embrace. Alerice wrapped her arms around Oddwyn's gentle spirit and was about to sob once more, but for some reason she felt her own soul voiding itself of angst.

Alerice glanced up at the King of Shadows and the Raven Queen, once again seated upon their thrones. They were not intervening to help her, and yet she felt she had the ability, indeed the empowerment, to withdraw from Oddwyn's embrace.

It was the Evherealme itself bolstering her. Alerice could sense it deeply within her. Somehow she felt in perfect tempo with this domain of endless time. Somehow it was a part of her, and she was a part of it.

Perhaps she had been blessed at birth. Perhaps Grammy Linden had known about it and never told her, but Alerice could not deny her love of shadows, where she had always felt the safest, and shadows were the very fabric of the Realme.

But more to the point, this everlasting master and mistress had not only offered her their weapons. They had offered her a new life, which was something Alerice now required. She could never return to her old life, for she could never return to Navre. If she were to walk again in the living world, she may as well do so in service to the Realme's king or queen, for at least then she would have the means to defend herself. Also, if these two wished her to willingly enter into service, she had the 'coin' to buy what she now wanted more than anything.

Alerice patted Oddwyn's shoulder and then stepped up toward the dais.

"Rulers of the Realme," she said. "I don't understand any of this, but I do believe wholeheartedly that the Reef killed me on the road. If that is so, then everything you are telling me must also be true, and though I have no idea what you will demand of me if I swear to you, I ask for only one thing in return."

The King of Shadows leaned forward, the upturned corner of his lips belying his affirmation that all mortals had their price. Alerice noted that the queen did not shift her posture, but was certainly focused.

"I ask that you protect my family," Alerice said. "And I hope that I may see them again one day, but only if it's safe."

"That's what you want?" the king asked. "Nothing more?"

"Nothing more, Your Majesty," she said. "For I wish nothing for myself." Alerice looked between them again as she considered her choice.

"Sir," she said to the king. "I appreciate that you wish to inspire me, for wicked people should face justice. However, I would prefer them to be measured as the Raven Queen has measured me. Let her apportion justice. I do not wish to."

The King of Shadows sat back while the Raven Queen leaned in. Her knowing smile and her head raised in pride provided Alerice with the clear answer of which weapon to accept. She took a solid step before the queen and knelt down on both knees.

"And so if you will protect my family, I will take up your dagger, in place of my own."

***

"Well, don't you cut a sleek figure," Oddwyn said, his ice-blue eyes dancing.

"Do I?" Alerice asked.

"Mmmm," Oddwyn replied.

The two stood in a grove of thick-trunked trees, the leafed branches of which stretched out overhead. The Raven Queen had restored Alerice to her mortal body, which Alerice had not been comfortable with at first.

After all, the vow of service had been an unnerving experience. The Raven Queen had risen from her throne and appeared before her. She had offered her dagger for Alerice to take, but as soon as Alerice had gripped its smooth, black handle, the Raven Queen had placed one hand over hers and her other palm atop Alerice's brow. Then she had guided the dagger's pommel over Alerice's breast in order to form a connection between mind and heart.

Alerice had felt the queen's power fill her. She had heard the queen ask, "Will you obey me, and act in my name? Will you remain steadfast to me as I remain steadfast to you? If these are your choices, swear upon your soul that they are."

Alerice was not certain of any formal response, so she repeated the queen's words. "These are my choices, and I do swear upon my soul."

After that, Alerice had felt her mind swirl. A strange sense of transition had overtaken her, as though she moved through multiple windows. Within each window she sensed a different world that she felt she could revisit and explore. She had heard voices whispering to her, voices she felt could guide and advise her, and when the swirling was over, she had felt the Raven Queen withdraw and saw Oddwyn approach to take hold of her and lift her up off her knees.

"Take her to the Convergence," the queen had said. "And lay her down."

"Yes, Great Lady Raven," Oddwyn had replied.

From there it had been a matter of helping Alerice settle back down within her body. The Raven Queen had accompanied them to the Convergence, and as soon as Alerice had stepped into her flesh as she might step into a long, thin sack, sat down, and lay back, the Raven Queen had instructed her to close her eyes.

When next Alerice opened them, while drawing in a deep breath, she had risen up whole and sound. Both the queen and Oddwyn had smiled, and then the Raven Queen had told Oddwyn to 'proceed'.

"I can't really see myself, you know," Alerice said as she ran her palms down the sides of her newly fitted tunic of black metal scales. Each scale lay flat along her body. The tunic buckled closed on either side, and Oddwyn had helped Alerice don the armor, which remarkably felt no heavier than a bodice.

The tunic spanned Alerice's torso from her neck to the width of her hips, and should she require more outfitting, Oddwyn had also offered her pauldrons and a gorget. She had refused the extra gear, for the tunic would easily suffice. After all, she could not imagine the Raven Queen sending her into battle.

Oddwyn buckled a black belt about Alerice's waist that was studded with the same white metal that composed the queen's crown. Apparently, it was a Realme amalgam that had only rarely seen the light of the living world. The queen's dagger, a Realme weapon, rested in a sheath affixed to the belt, and Alerice found her hand naturally drifting toward it. She gripped its handle, and then ran her fingers about its hilt.

"I'm glad you chose the dagger," Oddwyn said. "A sword would never suit you, although you should see the king's blade in action. If you throw it, it will always strike the target. Then all you have to do is hold your hand high overhead, and it will reappear in your palm."

Alerice smiled and drew her Realme dagger. It appeared to be a common blade, and yet as she gazed upon it, she could see shifting lines shimmer and flux. Indeed, the blade felt alive.

"Does this also reappear in your palm?" she asked.

"Yes, and it will always strike its mark as well, but it will also guide you to the target that most requires striking. That may surprise you when the time comes, but trust in the blade's integrity. That's my one piece of advice."

"Oddwyn, my friend," Alerice said with a smile. "I seriously doubt you ever limit yourself to one piece of advice."

Oddwyn regarded her and then offered, "It depends on what the advice is. Sometimes I only say things once. But there's something else the blade can do. Look at it more closely."

Alerice did, and soon saw that the blade's shifting lines blended into a surface that brightened before the weapon presented the scene of her family in Uncle Judd's home.

Alerice could see her own face reflected in the dagger's surface even as she gazed upon the sight of her loved ones stricken with worry. The Reef must have made good on his promise to return her dagger, and her family must have discovered it. She could see Cousin Chessy along with his younger brothers, Clancy and Little Judd, pacing about, longing to take action. She saw Uncle Judd argue with them and Aunt Carol pleading with them. Grammy Linden sat with Millie, both keeping out of the fracas.

"Try saying something to them," Oddwyn

suggested. "There's a good chance they can hear you whispering in their heads."

"Really?" she asked, hopeful that this might be true. Oddwyn simply gave her a slow, reassuring blink, and so Alerice focused on the blade.

"Millie?" she called, figuring that her cousin-in-law would be the most receptive. As she watched, she could see Millie's expression change as though listening. "Tell them I'm safe. Tell them that I escaped the Reef. Tell them I will send them a sign not to worry. I love you all, Millie. Don't let the boys do anything foolhardy. Make them listen. I know you can."

The blade brightened again, and then returned to its proper hue.

"You can't do that for too long, or do it too often, so save the moment for when you truly need it. In the meantime..." Oddwyn presented Alerice with a small crossbow.

"It looks like a toy."

"Well, it shoots like a spitting serpent," Oddwyn said. "And it will always have a bolt ready for you. Try it."

"Very well," Alerice said as she took hold of the bow. It was half the size of a proper crossbow, and as light as a child's plaything. Yet as Alerice hefted it to aim at a tree, the bow string pulled back of its own accord, and a glimmering black bolt appeared in the flight groove.

"Nice trick," Alerice exclaimed.

She squeezed the trigger into the tiller, and the bolt *whizzed* out with surprising speed. It struck the tree's trunk, and dissipated in a burst of dark light. Alerice stood silent in surprise, and then regarded the weapon.

"The bolts can kill most anyone in Mortalia or the Realme," Oddwyn said.

"Most anyone?" Alerice asked.

Oddwyn cocked his head. "You had best prepare yourself for an adventure, Alerice of Navre. You have no idea how long the Raven Queen has been awaiting a champion. I dare say that she has a long list of tasks in mind, and not all the personages on her list are going to be mortally wounded by a bolt from your bow."

Alerice lowered the weapon, wondering what to do with it. Oddwyn's countenance changed into that of a maiden, who gestured for Alerice to give it to her.

"It goes here," she said in her soft voice as she unbuttoned a strap on Alerice's belt and slipped the crossbow in so that the catch rested on the opposite hip from the Realme dagger.

Alerice regarded the Realme's Herald, and then could not help but ask, "Oddwyn, why do you keep doing that?"

"Doing what?" Oddwyn asked as she stood and looked Alerice over.

"...Changing hairstyles," Alerice said, deciding that a euphemism would be the most tactful way of addressing the fluctuations in gender.

"Do you wish to take issue with my expression?" Oddwyn asked matter-of-factly as she raised an eyebrow.

"Well, I'd be lying if I said I wasn't curious."

Oddwyn sighed through her nose. "Mortals... Very well. For me, there are times when the headiness of youthful moments best conveys my strongest self. Then there are times when I embrace the softness of my soul. I am a spirit of both reflections and quite happy to move between them."

"But, it's rather confusing."

"To you. But that's because you expect to see something specific when you look upon me. Perhaps when you do look at me, you should prepare yourself to see something different than what you expect. I see no reason to change myself in order to suit you or anyone else."

Alerice was about to mull this over, for no one had ever put the matter of personal identity so plainly before. However, a swirling ether of black, midnight blue, and deep teal appeared between two tree trunks, and the Raven Queen appeared in an opening portal.

She stepped forward into the grove. "Oddwyn," she said.

Oddwyn curtseyed, smiled at Alerice's outfitting, and then moved gracefully to the portal, where she stepped through. The queen banished the ether, and bade Alerice to accompany her.

The Raven Queen led Alerice to the edge of a rise overlooking a road. They stood in the hill country where the highs and lows of the landscape rolled out as far as the eye could see. Upon the hills, Alerice could see more stands of trees, terraced fields, and vineyards.

"I am sending you to the town of Basque," the queen stated. "Your first task it to slay a beast of two faces that has recently begun to feed upon innocent souls."

Alerice looked up at her matron. "I'm sorry, what?"

The Raven Queen stood tall as she gazed into the distance. A flock of ravens flew in and circled about her head. She raised a willow-white hand to greet them, and they alighted on to it one by one before they flew to the ground at her feet.

Alerice made a mental note that a group of such birds was commonly known as an 'unkindness', but then a group of crows was also known as a 'murder'. How wrong the common folk were to have named a flock of any black birds in such a manner.

"My Queen?" Alerice said. "You ask me to slay a beast with two faces? Doesn't that seem the stuff of fancy?"

"The beast is hidden," the queen said in her voice of dark honey. "You can expose it if you trust in yourself, but it must die and you must be the one to kill it."

"Does it breathe fire or fly or do any beast-like things I should know about?" Alerice asked. She was attempting to be sincere, but as she heard her own words, she could not help but think how ridiculous this all seemed.

"Use the weapons I have given you. Use your good judgment, and use this, for now that you are mine, I mark you as such."

Alerice was not certain what the queen meant, and she nearly startled as the Raven Queen turned to her. Then the queen appeared directly before her. Alerice stood straight as the Raven Queen took her cheeks in her palms and lifted her face up toward hers. Then the Raven Queen kissed Alerice on the brow.

Alerice experienced the same mental fluctuations that she had when swearing her allegiance to the queen, and she required a moment to gain control of her senses, even after the queen had concluded her kiss. The queen floated backward to allow Alerice some space as Alerice felt a pulsing sensation upon her brow

She drew her Realme dagger to see her reflection. An iridescent black mark now appeared to be inked onto her forehead. At the center rested a short, thin oval with a pointed bottom tip and capped with a dot. From either side, S-curls fanned out, much like the shape of bird's wings.

The Raven Queen held up her willow-white hand, and the mark began to glow. At once, Alerice could see the town of Basque as though her spirit was being thrust toward it. She saw herself standing within the town's central square, and then she saw herself looking at the backside of a building, which Alerice thought was an inn or public house.

Then Alerice startled awake to find that the Raven Queen had vanished. She stood alone on the rise, looking along the road below and knowing that she had a long walk ahead of her.

Just then, Alerice heard a horse neigh and snort, and she turned about to find a magnificent black mount. It was not as tall or bulky as a plow horse, nor was it as sleek as a strider. It stood at a height Alerice considered to be perfect for her. Its mane, tail, and feathered fetlocks were luxurious, and Alerice knew from their glossy sheen that this animal was another gift from the Realme.

The horse bore black tack studded with the queen's white metal. It shook its head, waiting for Alerice to approach. She sheathed her dagger and walked up to the creature, knowing that they were bonded on this, the first of many tasks.

The horse nickered and pressed its head to Alerice's shoulder. She scratched it behind the ears, and then saw a pair of black gauntlets draped over the saddle horn. She pulled them on, noting that they fit perfectly. She moved the reins over the horse's neck and prepared to mount, but then she felt the mark upon her brow activate and heard the Raven Queen's voice ring clearly in her mind.

"This is your Realme pony, for my champion does not walk. You may name him whatever you wish."

"Oh, that's easy," Alerice said as she mounted and took hold of the reins. "Come on, Jerome. Let's go to Basque."

***

Alerice had been riding throughout the day, and evening was drawing in. A while back she had thought it strange that the Raven Queen had not placed her closer to Basque, but as the day had progressed she had made good use of the time by testing Jerome's gaits. His trot had been surprisingly comfortable. His canter had covered much more distance than Alerice had expected, and his gallop had been by far the most exhilarating experience Alerice had ever known. She had felt as though she had flown as he ran, and she couldn't be certain if she hadn't. Who knew what a Realme pony was capable of, and she was only too happy to find out.

In the end, Alerice had settled into a walk, for she did not wish to spend Jerome needlessly. She had hoped Basque was only one more day's ride away, but she had no frame of reference regarding the distance for she had not encountered any other riders on her journey.

Trees lined the roadside, which comforted Alerice, for they provided ample shadows to protect her should the need arise. True, she now possessed weapons and armor, but she did not know the use of them nearly as well as she knew her beloved shadows.

She wondered where to make camp and what goods lay in store in Jerome's saddlebags, but she noticed a faint glow ahead and decided to take the chance that she might come across a helpful person who had also stopped for the evening.

Alerice approached a small campfire burning in a makeshift pit, and reined Jerome to a halt. Whoever had lit the fire had piled some rocks about it to form a ring, and had crafted a spit on which roasted a good-sized rodent. However, that person was nowhere to be found, and Alerice was not certain of the best course of action.

She removed one of her gauntlets and placed her palm on Jerome's shoulder. She trusted in his ability to sense things she could not, and as the horse did not appear to be nervous, she decided to take the initiative.

"Hello?" she called. Her voice faded into the trees, but no one responded. She decided to throw caution to the wind, and dismount. Then she paced to the fire pit, and looked about.

"Hello?" she called again.

Alerice heard the scrape of a sword being drawn, and turned about to find a man standing in the shadows not far from her. He leveled his blade but did not approach. Alerice took confidence in the fact that she bore ranged weapons, and if he decided to attack, she would have the advantage.

"Good evening to you. My name is..." Would it matter if she used her true name? Basque was nowhere near Navre, so the Reef could not possibly reach her here. Besides, she now had the Raven Queen's protection. "My name is Alerice Linden. May I join you tonight?"

The man hesitated before he stepped forward, broadsword still leveled. He was of a good height with strong shoulders. His weather-worn tunic bore a military cut, and Alerice noted a regimental badge of a broadsword set point-down between two bull's horns on the upper-left chest. He sported a wide-brimmed hat, which Alerice wondered was customary for the local folk. His salt-and-pepper hair did not quite reach his shoulders.

The man paced toward Alerice, who continued to judge the distance between them, and then paused to look her over. Alerice could see his hazel eyes dart from her black scale mail to her dagger and crossbow to Jerome. Then the man's shoulders dropped and he exhaled a single, dejected word. "Damn."

"Why damn?" Alerice asked.

The man sighed, somewhat crestfallen, and then sheathed his sword. He looked Alerice over once more, and then folded his arms across his chest as though resigned to fate.

"Do you speak?" she asked.

"Yes," he answered.

His voice belied the firmness of an experienced

man of action, and Alerice had no doubt that this fellow had seen many battles. She smiled at him, for a man of honor would not harm her. Of course, she did not know if he was a man of honor, for he was clearly not assigned to any present service.

"May I ask your name?" she said.

His lips smacked open, but he still did not speak. Then he glanced about at the fire and the short grass and seemed to decide there was enough room for two.

"Kreston," he said. "Kreston Dühalde. Unsaddle your horse and sit down if you like."

Alerice eased her stance. She nodded before she crossed over to Jerome and led him off the road. Unbuckling his bridle and removing his bit were simple tasks. Jerome even lowered his head so that she could reach. Ungirthing his saddle, however, was another matter, for she had not fastened it in the first place, and it did not seem to loosen with any ease.

Kreston watched her efforts, and then crossed over to her. He nudged her aside, and with a few quick motions, he loosed the girth strap, hefted the saddle off Jerome's back, and plopped it down. He also handed Alerice the saddlebags as he looked at her with a slight scold in his expression.

"You look like you've done that before," she said.

"When you've saddled as many horses as I have, it's second nature. Let me know if you want help getting him ready in the morning."

"Where's your mount?" she asked.

Kreston head-gestured to the trees, where Alerice could make out a stallion's outline safely sequestered among the trunks. She nodded again and moved her arm under Jerome's jaw to place a palm on his cheek to guide him in the same direction.

"Always keep your mount hidden when you can," Kreston advised. "That way an enemy will think you can't flee."

"That's good advice," she said. "I suspect you've known as many enemies as you have horses."

He straightened and looked at her. "Yes."

"You have got to be joking," Kreston said with a chuckle. "A two-headed beast? In Basque?"

Alerice giggled despite herself. "I know, but I have this... this matron, and that's what she told me to look for. It's absurd, but I've recently come to appreciate absurdity."

"You must have," he said. "Now, what is this stuff?"

Alerice regarded the bottle she had pulled from one of her saddlebags. "I have no idea. Let's just call it Realme Brew."

"Realme Brew? Now that's a first."

"For me too, and I've seen just about every bottle there is."

Alerice and Kreston had both decided to take their ease, and the bottle certainly helped dissolve any wariness. Alerice wondered if Oddwyn had supplied it, for she suspected that both he, and she, was a spirit who enjoyed mortal brews.

They had shared the roasted rodent and filled their cups, and soon it would be time for sleep. However, with at least one drink remaining, they had decided to chat.

"So where do you hail from, Alerice Linden?"

"Oh, I'd rather not speak of it. You?"

"Álava originally," Kreston said. "But I didn't stay there long. My father was a bastard, and my family blamed me for crippling my mother in childbirth, so I left for the army and never looked back."

"And you fought and won?"

"I fought. I didn't always win."

A moment passed as Kreston recalled a memory, but then Alerice watched him look her over. She looked down at her armor, noting how her scales glistened in the firelight.

"Who'd've thought that a maid as comely as you would don a tunic like that," he said. "Your hair, Alerice. Your smile."

Alerice hid an appreciative grin.

"How I wish you weren't wearing it, though," he said. "You must have such a lovely breast."

"Must I?" she asked coyly. "And what would be the good of it to you?"

"Alerice Linden, I've learned to live in the moment. You're a handsome lass, make no mistake. Enjoy the compliment, for I'll go no further." He drained his cup and then set it down so that he could fold his fingers behind his head and gaze up at the stars. “But if you had a bodice in that pack, I certainly wouldn’t mind if you wore it instead of all those scales.”

“Well, this has become comfortable, actually, and I’d rather keep it on.”

“Suit yourself,” he said.

The dying fire crackled, and the embers illuminated the circle of rocks. Alerice finished her cup and looked about for a place to curl up. She had found a cloak inside Jerome’s saddlebag, and she folded herself within it, noting that it suited her as much as her bed’s blanket back at the Cup and Quill.

“Never get comfortable,” Kreston cautioned.

“What?” she asked.

“Never get comfortable. The day you think you are in command of your world is the day that your world comes shattering down. Have you ever taken a first watch? Maybe you should try it to get into the habit.”

Alerice sat up, noting the road and the stand of trees nearby. “Do you think someone will happen upon us?”

Kreston likewise sat up. “Someone can always happen upon you. Some ‘thing’ can always happen. The question is, are you ready when it does?”

Alerice could not help but recall the night of Gotthard’s rape and Cousin Jerome’s death. Then she recalled the moment of the Reef’s attack that had ended her life, and emotions welled up against her will.

Kreston sat up more alert and leaned in toward

her. "Hey, sorry. I didn't mean to spark a bad thought."

"It's all right," she said. "There's nothing to be done about it now, except serve my matron, I suppose."

"She sounds like a cooky, old bat. A two-headed beast."

Alerice nodded to hide her grief, and watched Kreston get to his feet and take a stance.

"So how do you know if it's any good?" he asked.

"How do I know if what's any good?" she replied.

"Your armor. How do you know if it's worth anything when it truly counts?"

"Ummm, I suppose I don't."

"You mean you've never tested it?"

"No, and if I told you how little a time I've had it, you wouldn't believe me."

Kreston smirked and looked about the ground. He found a tree branch and hefted it as he might heft his broadsword.

"Let's test it."

Alerice regarded him and doffed her cloak to stand up. "Here and now?"

"No better time," he said. "I promise, no leg or head blows. You're not wearing a helm, and your leggings have no scales. Torso only. Yes, Alerice Linden?"

Alerice didn't mind the challenge. She had deliberately drunk half of what Kreston had drunk, and this was not the first time a man wanted to roughhouse with her. After all, she had grown up with four male cousins.

Alerice stood before Kreston. There was something about him that she trusted, though she was not certain why.

"Very well," she said. "Let's have a blow."

"First, a gut jab," he said to prepare her. "Someone will always want to stick you like a pig when you're in a melee."

He aimed the branch at her midsection and thrust. He did not fully pull his blow, and the impact knocked Alerice's breath out. However, the armor proved itself and she recovered her stance, waiting for more.

"Good scales," he said. "Now, how about a side shot? I'll wager that this two-headed beast has arms that will splay you out if given the chance."

Alerice watched Kreston pull the branch back and then swing for her liver. His blow was true and she fell aside to her knee, but the armor prevented any injury. She coughed and stood.

"You don't give up easily, do you?" he said as he swung for her opposing hip.

This time Alerice dodged the blow by shifting her stance just enough for the branch to pass her by. Kreston swung through, and as she saw his surprise that he had missed his mark, she rammed her shoulder into him and knocked him to the grass.

Kreston recovered and jumped to his feet to face her, but his hazel eyes seemed to go wild. He swung for her side again, but then redirected his blow to swing for her head.

"Kreston," Alerice said as she ducked. "You said no head blows."

"Shut up, Landrew!" Kreston shouted to some invisible person at his side as he swung for Alerice's legs. "I'll get the men out of this! Just take the damned hill!"

"Kreston," Alerice said, clearing some distance between them. "Who are you talking to?"

"I told you to shut up, Lieutenant!" he roared. "Take the hill, you little sack of shite!"

"Kreston," Alerice called, clearing more space. She watched him engage in a one-sided battle against foes who must have seemed real in his mind, and waited until he had spent the last of his energy flailing the branch about.

In a short while, he fell to the grass, panting, and as he finally dropped the branch, Alerice felt it was safe enough to approach him.

He clutched his side as if wounded. He reached for something in the distance, and stifled a cry of, "Landrew."

Alerice retrieved the branch and gently pressed it into Kreston's shoulder.

"Kreston?"

"Damn it," he muttered. "Damn it." He glanced at her, though he did not seem to know who she was, and stammered, "They're all dead, Field Marshal. They couldn't take the hill."

"Kreston," she said with a firmer shove. "It's Alerice. I'm here with you on the road to Basque. There's no one else about."

Kreston began to rub his head through his wide-brimmed hat, pressing harder and harder until he clutched the leather and pressed it into his skull. Then his eyes snapped open and he startled as he looked about. He looked up at Alerice and scrambled to his feet.

"Get away from me!" he shouted. She did not, and he locked stares with her to say, "Alerice Linden, get as far away from me as you can. Forget you ever met me. Ride away and never look back. Whatever you seek in Basque, find it on your own."

Alerice still did not move. Kreston snarled and then stepped forward to strike her on the jaw hard enough to fell her to the grass, dazed.

Alerice did her best to regain her senses, but as Kreston bolted for the trees, she was aware of one thing. He had jumped onto his horse's bare back and dug in his heels to ride away into the night.

***

Alerice had not seen Kreston the next morning. He had not returned, and Alerice knew that it was not best to wait for him.

Her dreams had been a constant vision of Basque as the Raven Queen had presented it when kissing her brow, moving quickly toward the waiting town, standing within the central square, and standing behind the building she now knew was a public house.

She had woken alone, wrapped in the safety of her cloak. She had glanced about to find Jerome, who was enjoying some sweet grass near the base of the trees. Kreston had left his horse's tack behind, along with his own saddlebags, and Alerice had decided to cover them with some fallen branches in hopes that no one might discover them until he returned to claim them.

Her jaw ached from his punch, but she bore him no ill will, for she knew that when a man was haunted by 'battlefield voices', he was not always the master of his own mind.

The journey to Basque had only required half the day. Alerice was aware of the figure she presented, a blonde woman dressed in black scales riding a prancing black mount. Farmers had gawked and folk had pointed, but she had kept her eyes forward as she made for the town.

Folk had continued to whisper about her and shuffle away when she gazed upon them, and so having no idea where to begin her search for a two-headed beast, she did what all inquiring travelers do – head for the busiest tavern.

In Basque, this was the Pink Rose.

Alerice felt strange entering, for the moment she had crossed the threshold, she recalled each time a notable personage had stepped foot inside the Cup and Quill. She had been able to take the measure of nearly every one of them – be he a rowdy local, a well-established merchant, or a man of war and fortune. She tried to put the last image out of her mind as she paced in, for it reminded her of Kreston.

Knowing that she would be the topic of town gossip for weeks to come, she decided to give the people a good show, and so she held her head high as she found an empty table near two men playing cards.

The first one looked up twice from his hand as she approached. He pointed to his gaming partner to do the same. They blinked with incredulity as she brushed aside her cloak and drew up a chair, and they began to snicker as she looked toward the bar for the master or mistress.

Alerice did not regard them as she rubbed her still-throbbing jaw, but as they openly displayed their scorn, she placed her crossbow and dagger on the table. She half-glanced in their direction, and then she jammed the dagger into the tabletop, causing it to flash brightly as it had when presenting the scene of Uncle Judd's home. She had not expected this to happen, but the surprise inspired the men to collect their cards and coins and move to another table.

"Well, aren't you a woman of mystery," the inn mistress said, coming forward with a full pint. "This one's on the house. We're going to have such traffic in here this evening if you return to join us that I don't mind advancing you a cup."

“Thank you,” Alerice said, taking a sip. The beer was watered down, and Alerice wondered if the people in Basque had ever known a decent cup of brew.

“My name is Arrosa,” the inn mistress said. “I’m known for the finest blooms in Basque. It’s my specialty.”

Alerice noted the carved roses painted bright pink that dotted the support beams and ceiling coffers. She spotted sprays of freshly cut roses decorating the bar.

Then her gaze fell onto a pretty young lass hurrying to bring a customer a goblet of wine. The girl could not have been more than twelve or thirteen, nearly the age Alerice had been when Uncle Judd had invited her to wait tables. It was natural for family establishments to employ their young ones, for how else should they learn their respective trades? Still, there was something about this girl that did not seem right.

Her complexion was a bit too pale. Her cheeks were a bit too pink, and her dark blonde curls were a bit too perfect. Alerice sensed resentment hiding behind the lassie’s forced smile, which she evidenced by tensing as the customer stroked the back of his finger along her face. Indeed, Alerice bristled upon seeing the gesture, for Uncle Judd would never have allowed any patron to express such familiarity with a young thing who was barely old enough to fill out her bodice.

"Ah, I see you've spotted my Honey," Arrosa said. "Honey," she beckoned to the girl.

Honey responded by hurrying to Arrosa's call. She stood before the inn mistress, who placed hands on her shoulders to turn her about and face the tavern's new guest.

Alerice watched as Honey slowly lifted her blue eyes. The girl's resentment became palpable as their gazes met, for Honey seemed to be thinking a poignant question. However, then Arrosa pressed her thumb into Honey's back and the lassie's face lit up with a beaming smile.

"Good day, black mistress," she said in a tiny voice as she offered a tiny curtsey.

Alerice wanted to reach out to Honey, for her façade of welcome could not disguise her apprehension at Arrosa's touch, but Arrosa bade Honey to resume her duties as she sent her to wait on other eager men.

"She's my eldest," Arrosa said. "Though I look after my brother's and sister's children as well. Some help me here, some work the stables behind. Since last year's blight, folks have had trouble feeding their families, and since Basque is on the crossroads to several cities, there's plenty of work for them to do here."

"I see," Alerice said, doing her best to maintain her guise as mysterious and aloof.

"Is the brew to your liking?"

"Mmmm," she replied as she took another sip.

Then she placed the tankard down, slid it to the side, and leaned in toward Arrosa. "Actually, I'm searching for something. I've heard a tale that there is a beast here in Basque. One with two faces, two heads. One that feeds off innocent souls."

Arrosa blinked and nearly laughed out loud, but Alerice rose up to stand tall before her. She projected the empowerment of her charge as a servant of the Evherealme, and though she was not certain how she managed it, she felt the Raven Queen's mark upon her brow pulse. As she watched the inn mistress' eyes widen, she was sure that the mark had flashed.

"This is my task," Alerice said in a voice of complete confidence. "And I shall not disappoint the matron who has sent me here."

"But..." Arrosa stammered, evidently uncertain what to say. "There is no beast. Beasts are cottage tales that grammies tell children to frighten them into doing their chores."

"Let me make myself clear," Alerice said, taking a half-step forward, which caused Arrosa to back away by the same measure. Inwardly, Alerice was chortling, for this farce was fast becoming hilarious, but outwardly she presented herself to be what the Raven Queen had outfitted her to be – her champion.

"Look at the mark on my brow. Look at my blade lodged in the table. I am a creature who knows other worlds, and if I say a beast dwells in Basque, I know of what I speak. You say you wish me to return here this evening..." Alerice looked about the tavern, noting that all eyes were fixed on her. "Then I shall, and I will find this two-headed creature, and I will save the innocents it threatens."

"Yes, mistress..." Arrosa said, though her voice trailed off for she did not know Alerice's name.

"Alerice, daughter of the Raven Queen."

"Raven's... daughter," Arrosa stammered as she curtseyed. "I will do my utmost to serve you." She looked twice toward the bar, her eyes landing on a man who had just appeared. "'Enri," she called. "Let's have another round for our guest."

"Let's have two," Kreston said.

Arrosa turned about to find him standing at her side, not at all certain of how he had approached without anyone having seen him.

Alerice brightened as she beheld him, but he maintained a character complementary of hers, and together they hid a knowing smile as the inn master hurried over with two tankards.

Kreston took a seat opposite Alerice and accepted the brew. Then he placed a coin on 'Enri's platter, and bade him to leave them in peace.

The tavern's collective gaze turned back to whatever had previously occupied them, and Alerice found herself blending comfortably into the shadows, Kreston following suit.

He looked her over, his intimidating demeanor melting into one of concern. He reached out to touch her jaw, noting the bruise he had inflicted and how she flinched the moment his fingertips brushed her skin.

"Oh damn it, Alerice," he said, his voice low. "I'm so sorry for last night."

"Kreston, what are you doing here?"

"I had to seek you out. I had to tell you that I never meant to hurt you, and I never would have laid a hand on you if I had been able to think clearly. But, I'm not always able to, you see, and striking you has been eating away at me since I did it. I knew where you'd be headed, and in a town like this, it's natural that this place would be your first stop. I just hope you can forgive--"

"I have already," she said, ending his plea. "Kreston, you're not the first military man I've met. My father died in Lord Andoni's southern campaigns. I remember a time when he brought home a wounded comrade and asked me to watch him one night. He told me not to get too close, because the man saw ghosts in his sleep, and I was only four.

"And he did see ghosts. And when he woke up, he cried out and ran for the back door, and my father had to catch him and help him see sense. So don't worry. You struck me because you feared you would harm me, and while you do pack a wallop, at least you didn't truly injure me."

Kreston looked her over, and then sat back. "You think about others a great deal, don't you?"

Alerice smiled, and sipped again from her mug. Then she spied something below the crown of his hat that she had not been able to see in the previous night's darkness.

"What's that mark on your forehead?"

"That's, uhh... Nothing. An old scar I earned doing something stupid."

It was not a large step for Alerice to link a scar on a man's brow and the blow that would have caused it, and from there to the madness of memory that such a blow might induce. She said nothing further as she sipped her brew once more.

Kreston took up his tankard and raised it to her before he drank – at which point he spat the brew onto the table and regarded the mug.

"That's the worst stuff I've had in years. How can you even drink it?"

"Practice," she mused.

Kreston moved the tankard aside and stood up. "Come on, let's go find your beast."

***

The sun had reached the western horizon as Alerice stood with Kreston in the town's central square. She felt as though she was completing a part of her envisioned task by doing so, but the simple act of surveying the town answered no questions. Rather, it clearly marked both Alerice and Kreston as strangers, and all folk in all towns bore a natural avoidance of anything as strange as a blonde woman in black scale armor and a tall man in a wide-brimmed hat bearing a broadsword.

Alerice had left Jerome in the stables behind the

Pink Rose, along with her cloak and gear. Kreston had done likewise with his mount. The two sported their weapons as they walked toward the door to a local chapel. It was dedicated to the brother deities Gäete, God of Storms, and L'Orku, God of Thunder, and Alerice thought it might be a good place to search out lore regarding a two-headed beast.

The chapel's headmaster invited them in, knowing he was in the presence of a woman who must know the Evherealme, but while he paid respect to Alerice and the great Raven Mother whom she served, he could spin no tales of a beast of Basque.

Rather, he wished to engage on a variety of other topics, including the queen herself and the King of Shadows, until both Alerice and Kreston had become quite bored with his pedantic prattles. Kreston took the initiative to impose his military countenance upon the scholar while insisting that Alerice attend an upcoming rendezvous with the night's spirits, for if she failed to appear and appease the gods below, the entire town might face the Realme's displeasure.

"Where did you invent a story like that?" Alerice asked Kreston as they quickly paced away from the closing chapel doors.

"Oh, you'd be surprised at some of the stories I know."

Alerice next stopped by an apothecary's shop to see if mixtures and magic could reveal any clues to the beast's whereabouts. However, she knew an odd-water shop when she saw one, and she could see that the apothecary himself was a curator of all things curious and nothing substantial.

Alerice decided on her own to leave before Kreston invented another story to explain their sudden egress.

"This isn't working, Kreston," Alerice said as they walked past the central square once more. She paused to take stock of the town's buildings, noting that windows shuttered as she gazed upon them. She was fast losing confidence in her ability to live up to the Raven Queen's expectations, but she was not certain if she should say anything to Kreston.

"I'd like to know your business," a man said from the side.

Both Alerice and Kreston turned to find the Reef of Basque approaching with a crew of five men. Alerice tensed, which Kreston seemed to sense, but she decided to cast a full bet that the Reef firstly, was not acquainted with the Reef of Navre, and secondly was the last man who could possibly point her in the direction of some two-headed monster.

"My name is Alerice, and I have been tasked to uncover a creature somewhere within your town. Now, before you laugh or consider me a madwoman, allow me to assure you that I am quite sincere, and I would greatly appreciate knowing whatever you might know about such a creature."

Some of the Reef's men chuckled, but the Reef

waved them to be silent as he stepped forward. He regarded the bruise on Alerice's jaw, but she held her head high as though it was a mark of service. Then he regarded Kreston's worn military tunic and its badge of a broadsword set point-down between two bull's horns.

"Crimson Brigade? King Kemen?"

Kreston nodded.

"Crimson Brigade?" Alerice asked, noting in the daylight that the emblem was, in fact, dark red. "I've heard of your ghost."

"Really," Kreston said.

"I heard things didn't go so well for your regiment," the Reef said.

"No, they didn't," Kreston said.

The Reef offered nothing further as he regarded Alerice.

"My fair woman, I appreciate your sincerity, so as a token of good will on behalf of my town, I will suggest that you make up your bed tonight and sleep well. Then I would have you take your leave in the morning. Whoever told you that a beast dwells here in Basque is either sending you on a fool's errand or is mad themself.

"There are no such things as beasts. They do not live in this humble place. I have been the Reef here for over a decade, and if a beast did exist, I would have already slaughtered it. Stories would have already circulated about my deeds, and the lore would have spread to wherever you are from."

Alerice thought the words over, seeing sense in them. Indeed, any story of any mythical creature being brought down by a courageous Reef would have reached Navre, no matter from how far away. Perhaps the Raven Queen was testing her faith with this task. Perhaps she wanted Alerice to follow her instructions blindly in order to present her with a true task sometime soon. The queen had promised Alerice a chance at self-forgiveness, and she had to admit that for the last day she had not been consumed by the guilt over poisoning Gotthard. Perhaps this was the reason to send her on a fool's errand.

Alerice placed a hand on the Reef's arm.

"Thank you for your advice, sir. Yes, my friend and I shall leave in the morning."

***

"I should have known better than to think I could do this, Kreston," Alerice said as she moved Jerome's saddle onto a patch of hay to make up a place to lie down. She could not bear to make another appearance in the Pink Rose that evening, and in her mind she was already riding away at dawn.

"You know, in my career," Keston said as he reclined against his own saddle, watching her, "I've made good decisions and I've made terrible ones, but the one thing I can hold as my own is knowing that most of my ideas were well-founded. In the long run, the better ideas outnumber the bad ones."

"I'm sure that's true," she said. "But you've had a career of life choices. I'm just a tavern maid. I can keep a ledger. I can inspire men to settle grievances over a pint. But I can't pretend to be I'm something I'm not."

"And what are you pretending to be?" he said, sitting up.

She humphed to herself. "You wouldn't believe me if I told you."

"I might."

"No, you wouldn't. I don't believe it much myself. Let's just say that the headmaster at the chapel was right when he recognized that I was in service to the Raven Queen. I mean, at least I think I am, but maybe I've actually gone mad since..."

She wanted to trace her actions back to Gotthard's attack, for indeed an act that savage could have made her mad. For all she knew, she had never been to the Realme at all. The Reef might not have actually killed her. Rather, she might be lying in bed at Uncle Judd's this very moment, suffering from some lasting delusion.

In all honesty, wasn't this more believable? The King of Shadows and the Raven Queen? Oddwyn and the Evherealme? Or a broken mind trying to console itself from Gotthard assaulting her and killing her beloved Jerome before her eyes.

"Alerice, what are you recalling?" Kreston asked.

"I don't want to think about it," she said, averting her eyes. "I just... I just want to wake up."

Kreston grimaced, and then threw hay into Alerice's face.

"Hey!" she exclaimed, but he threw another handful, and another. Then he stood up and started kicking hay onto her lap and legs.

"Kreston, what are you doing?"

"Seeing if you're awake," he said flatly as he kicked more hay into her hair. She got to her feet and pushed him away, but he pushed back, forcing her against a beam supporting the stable's roof.

"So, are you awake?" he demanded.

"Stop it, Kreston. If you're hearing battlefield voices right now, I'm sorry but I can't help you because I'm not in my own right mind."

"Father Fire, you're not!" he cursed. "And if I were hearing battlefield voices, you'd know it. Right now the only voice I'm hearing is yours, and all I see is a frightened little girl. You don't trust your senses. You don't trust yourself. I can't believe this is always how you've been. You're made of better stuff, so I'm thinking that something bad happened to you recently, and now you're falling apart when you need to form a plan and get the job done."

"What job? This is all fantasy. There is no beast here, let alone one with two heads that feeds on innocent souls."

"Damn it, Alerice, that's not what *she* said to you!"

Alerice froze. Then she straightened. "What *who* said to me?"

"*Her*," Kreston said with a sneer. "Sorry, I mean

Her Majesty. *She* did not say a two-headed beast. *She* said a beast with two faces."

Alerice stood stunned. "How do you know about the Raven Queen?"

Kreston sighed. "Oddwyn told me, and before you ask..."

He doffed his hat and ran his fingers through his salted brown bangs. What he had claimed was a scar was in fact a mark upon his brow that bore a striking similarity to Alerice's own, only his was a series of varying striations that looked as though they had been carved by fingernails.

"You?" Alerice asked. "You are the king's man that the Raven Queen mentioned."

"Yes," he said. "That's why I swore when I met you. Oddwyn told me that *she* had taken a new champion, so when I lit my fire by the roadside, I expected to meet someone like myself. I never expected *she* would choose a person who had clearly never seen a battle in her life."

"The queen said you did not serve the king well because you were a driven man, not one of good deeds."

"Oh, I serve the King of Shadows exactly the way he wants me to. Now if I were you, I'd think about what it is that you're supposed to find, because I can tell you that *she* is not to be denied."

Kreston hid a shudder that belied a past Alerice longed to discover. However, the Reef of Basque would force them both to leave in the morning, and now was not the time to pry him open.

"But what if I fail her?" she asked.

"*She'd* only send you back until you get it right. You pledged your soul, Alerice, and *she'll* never let you go. They never let you go, and they won't ever stop using you. You will belong to them for the rest of your life."

"You mean belong to her, to the queen, not to them both," she said. Kreston paused and then agreed. Again, Alerice knew there was more to him than he was allowing her to see. "I suppose I should reach out to her for guidance."

"If you do, I don't want to be anywhere nearby," Kreston said as he turned to leave. However, before he paced away, he turned back, a question clearly on his mind.

"Do you mind if I--"

"Please," Alerice offered.

"All right. What did you ask for? What did you get in exchange for taking the Realme's power?"

"How do you know I asked her for anything?"

"Alerice. Everyone who seeks them out asks for something."

"Did you?"

"Yes. I asked the King of Shadows for the power to defeat my enemies. He gave me that and more."

"And did that work well for you?" she asked.

"In some ways."

His reply only whetted her appetite to know more about him. However, she said, "Actually, I did not seek them out. Rather, they sought me. I had died and woken up in the Evherealme. Oddwyn brought me before them both. The queen told me that..."

"Everything had aligned at your birth, which is why you had always loved the shadows?"

Again, Alerice looked Kreston over. "You too?"

He nodded. She reached out to touch him, but he moved away.

"The queen offered me her dagger," Alerice continued, "and the king offered me his sword. They wanted me to choose."

"The king offered you his sword?" Kreston asked.

"Yes," she replied, but the consequences of that offering suddenly struck her. "And the queen reminded him that another mortal already bore it. If he had reclaimed his sword and given it to me, would that have affected you?"

"Probably," Kreston said.

Alerice thought it was best to refocus the conversation away from him. "Actually, I did ask for something."

"I knew it. What?"

"I asked for the queen to protect my family."

"That's all?"

"You know, the King of Shadows said the same thing. It's possible that I've been wrong in thinking better things of you, Kreston Dühalde. Perhaps you are his man, and well-suited to his tasks."

Kreston controlled a quick flash of anger, then turned away.

"Just summon *her* and figure things out," he said as he left the stables.

Alerice watched him go, but then sensed a presence off to the side.

"It's best to leave him be," Oddwyn said from the corner.

Alerice turned to find him. He stood near a rack of bridles, hands on his hips, one eyebrow raised.

"Kreston tries to help sometimes," Oddwyn continued. "But when he walks away, it's best to let him go. Trust me."

"Oddwyn, why didn't you tell me that the king's man was still alive and likely to find me?"

"Because that's not how the Raven Queen wished things, and I do what she wishes me to do, just as you need to do what she wishes you to do. And please, no more complaints. It's a waste of time."

Oddwyn advanced and reached out to brush Alerice's blonde bangs from her face. "You haven't really learned how to use this, now have you," he said, rubbing his thumb across the Raven Queen's mark. "It's time you learned."

Oddwyn flicked Alerice's brow quite roughly, activating the mark and forcing Alerice's spirit from her body. Oddwyn caught her limp figure and laid it down, even as he turned to her and said, "What are you waiting for? Go find what you seek."

Alerice wanted to ask what that was, but just as with the vision conveyed in the queen's kiss, she found her spirit pulled away from the stables and toward the backside of a building.

It was a public house, and the pink blooms in the nighttime garden informed Alerice of precisely which house. Her spirit hovered behind the Pink Rose, and as she floated closer she saw a familiar sight.

Arrosa was greeting men at the rear door. They slipped her coin, and she took their hats and cloaks. They had come for the company of 'busy lassies', a trade Alerice knew quite well from managing the Cup and Quill. However, as Alerice watched, she saw Arrosa produce Honey and offer her to one of the men.

The inn mistress was selling the company of a someone that young? Knowing she needed to see more, Alerice flew into the back rooms of the Pink Rose. She did not question how she traveled, but rather allowed her intuition to guide her – and what she found appalled her. Arrosa and 'Enri were putting all the young ones, lads and lassies, to work as company for men who were eager to have them. They could do nothing but accept their fate. Some even bore sprays of Arrosa's pink blossoms as they walked to their bed chambers.

It suddenly struck Alerice that the tavern's name was not chosen for the flowers, but for the young flesh sold, for the innocent souls so horribly abused, all under the direction of two schemers who certainly deserved to be held accountable.

"Oddwyn!" Alerice called, hoping Oddwyn might

help her return to her body. “Oddwyn, can you hear me?”

Alerice sensed no reply, and though she was fairly certain that she could return to her body on her own, she realized that she needed help to see this matter through. She pressed her lips together, and commanded herself to seek out Kreston.

Kreston stood beside a building, his sword in hand. He threw the blade into the building’s half-timber, where it lodged deeply. Then he held his hand high overhead. The sword appeared within his grasp, and Kreston prepared to throw it again.

“Stop that, will you,” Alerice called to him.

Kreston froze. “Alerice?” he called, looking about.

She was not certain how to present her spirit in the living world, and so she drew near to him – and flicked the mark of the King of Shadows scratched upon his brow.

Kreston reacted to the strike by backing a few steps, then he stood straight and activated the mark himself to extend his own spirit toward her. He did not venture out from his own body, lest he collapse, but he did lock stares with her.

“Alerice, what is it?”

“The inn master and mistress. They are selling their young ones for pleasure. Hurry and get the Reef. I will go help Honey and the others.”

Alerice flew away, not hearing Kreston’s warning that the Pink Rose was certain to have men protecting it.

***

Alerice settled down into her body, and then forced herself to draw in a deep breath as she opened her eyes. She exhaled and sat up, taking stock of her composure.

She was whole and sound. The comfort of her black scales bolstered her as did the Evherealme itself. She dove through Kreston's thrown hay for her belt, and securing it, she buckled it about her waist so that her weapons hung at her sides.

***

Alerice crept out from the stables, staying in the safety of the shadows. Arrosa greeted what appeared to be the evening's last lonely man, and as she closed the rear door, Alerice crept further forward.

She did not have a plan, apart from forcing Arrosa and her husband to surrender the young ones. Would this work? Would they harm the lads or lassies if the moment became dire? Did the Reef already know of their business and condone it?

Alerice put the last thought from her mind. The Reef must be a better man than that, for only a horrendous person could condone the nightwork of the Pink Rose. Besides, the Raven Queen had said the 'beast' of Basque had *begun* to feed upon innocent souls, so the Pink Rose's trade must be new. Even Arrosa had said that the young ones had come in since last year's blight. She would give the Reef a chance to prove himself, and if he did not, she would take some other action to get the young ones to a safe place.

For now, the rear door. Alerice saw that she must step out from the shadows to reach it, for two lanterns burned brightly on either side of the jamb. She must be quick, or she would be seen--

"Who are you?" a man called out.

Alerice turned and found one of the two men who had been playing cards. She stepped forward to confront him, uncertain if she should draw her dagger or crossbow.

"You're that little puffed-up nothing from this afternoon," he said. "Hey boys," he called over his shoulder. "Here's that little black bird I was telling you about."

Alerice watched as three more men came forward, and though she could see they meant to attack her, she found her senses rankling at being referred to as a 'bird' by yet another man confident of his own domination.

She stood her ground, unbuttoning the leather strap holding her crossbow. She hefted and leveled it. The bow string drew back of its own accord, and a gleaming black bolt appeared in the flight groove.

"What's that supposed to be?" the lead man demanded as all four encroached. "The little bird has a toy bow."

Alerice hesitated, not because she wasn't prepared

to fight, but because she had never been faced with a moment of kill or be killed. This was not the same as poisoning Gotthard. This was taking a life in order to protect her own, and she searched for the cool clarity that Kreston must have possessed in his many battles.

She fired into the lead man's shoulder.

"Father Fire!" he swore as the bolt sank into him and burst into a dark flash that knocked him to the ground.

Alerice watched him growl in agony. She had aimed the shot to wound him in hopes that his accomplices would flee. However, two men locked stares on her and charged.

Alerice lifted her crossbow again, but before she could shoot, a broadsword's point erupted through one man's chest, splattering his blood across her black scales.

The other man skidded to a stop and turned, only to find Kreston holding his hand high and his broadsword reappearing in his grasp. Kreston leveled the point and then drew back to throw, but the fellow – apparently possessing some amount of wit – ran off into the night, the fourth man following him.

Kreston advanced, stepping on the leg of the wounded man as he strode toward Alerice. They regarded one another then glanced down at their foe. The lead man – likewise possessing a decent modicum of sense – scrambled away in the opposite direction.

***

The rear door to the Pink Rose opened into the back hall, admitting Alerice and Kreston.

"I told you to summon the Reef," she said in a low voice.

"I did," he said, ice in his veins as he focused on the task at hand.

She led the way to the bottom of a staircase and gestured for Kreston to remain while she crept upward. Kreston watched her ascend, but then caught sight of two young lads and beckoned them to come to him for protection.

Alerice made her way along the upper hall, noting the closed doors. She would need to find the inn master or mistress before she hurried any young ones down to Kreston, for she could not risk the couple injuring any of the remaining girls or boys.

"I don't know what you think you've come for," 'Enri said from behind.

Alerice turned and saw him emerge from a door she had just passed.

"And I don't know who you think you are," he continued, "but you're leaving now, or I promise you that more than one of our little beauties will pay for it."

'Enri held no hostage, but he had the same look Gotthard had sported when striding into the Cup and Quill. What gave a man such a delusional predisposition? How dare he claim anyone to be his?

"Beast," she growled.

"Is that the best you can say?" the inn master chuckled.

Alerice's hand moved toward her dagger, which seemed ready to jump into her grasp. She turned her hip slightly so that 'Enri could not see her draw it, but suddenly one of the men who had come to purchase a young one's company ventured into the hall on Alerice's opposing side.

He charged forward, and she threw the dagger into his heart. This time, she had no hesitation about doing what needed to be done. This time she was ready to take a wicked life that was threatening not only hers but the lives of innocents – a decision reinforced when she saw a girl Honey's age hurry to the door and cry out at seeing the dead man's rolled-up eyes.

Alerice rushed to the lassie and hid her from view even as she raised her hand. Her dagger appeared in her palm, and she threw it into 'Enri's throat, killing him.

One face of the monster slain. One more to find.

Alerice descended the stairs, the lassie and several others in tow. She took stock of Kreston, who had gathered a few more lads, and prepared to leave by the rear door. However, as she bade the young ones to be silent, Alerice heard voices in the now-closed tavern.

She made her way through to the front of the house, appearing in the shadows of the bar.

"You know?" the Reef said to Arrosa.

Alerice saw the Reef's five men as well, but watched the inn mistress play the moment with cool lubricity.

"There have been several of us who have turned blind eyes to the rumors we have heard," the Reef continued. "Largely because none of us could imagine a thing so rotten as selling your young ones for pleasure."

"And you would take the word of strangers over mine?" Arrosa said. "We know one another, Darmond. Don't believe tales that will damage your reputation when they prove false."

"Prove false?" Alerice said as she advanced. "I'll show you what's true." Alerice turned back to see Kreston leading his group forward. She crouched down and held out her hand. "Come here, Honey. No one's going to hurt you ever again. You have my promise on that."

Kreston urged Honey to take a few steps forward, but the lassie gained confidence the moment she gripped Alerice's hand.

In that moment, Alerice understood the palpable sensation of Honey's initial resentment. When they had first met, the girl had indeed been thinking a poignant question, and it was undoubtedly, "Why are you letting bad things happen to us? Why don't you protect us?"

Well, now Alerice was. She drew Honey in and held her close to steady her, even as she leveled a stare at Arrosa, who in her eyes was viler than Gotthard.

Honey took a step on her own, gazing up at Arrosa. Then her blue eyes narrowed and she spat on the floor before returning to Alerice's side, where she pressed in.

"There's at least a dozen of them, Reef," Alerice said. "Arrosa and her husband likely collected them from parents unable to care for them. They are the proof of her crime."

"And her husband's," the Reef said. "Where is 'Enri?"

"Dead," Alerice stated in a voice of complete confidence. "Along with another man upstairs."

"You killed them?" the Reef asked.

This time, the empowerment that Alerice displayed was no charade. This time, she projected the bearing of someone who knew she was in the right, in the charge of the Raven Queen herself, and in holding the Reef's gaze, Alerice became well aware, that he was well aware, of this fact.

The Reef ordered one of his men to take hold of Arrosa and remove her via the front door, through which he and his crew had entered and remained open. Then he regarded the young ones.

"Right now, this is the safest place for them. There's no room for them at the constabulary, and it's obvious that you intend to protect them. I'll send food and blankets, and we'll see what we can do for them in the morning."

The Reef sent one of his men to clean up upstairs, and ordered the remaining three to guard the Pink Rose throughout the rest of the evening.

The Reef began to exit the tavern, but turned back. "Thank you. Apparently there was a beast here in Basque. I should have believed the stories that people had begun to tell me."

***

Alerice rubbed her bruised jaw as she watched Kreston load the last of the lads and lassies onto a hay wagon. Docents from the chapel dedicated to Imari, Mother Goddess of Water and Wind, were busily sorting things out with the Reef prior to departing. They had come forward to see to the welfare of each child, and they were settling finalities as they prepared to depart.

Kreston looked over at Alerice and smiled. He held his hat in hand, and was about to cross over to her, but he suddenly froze and looked past Alerice's shoulder.

Alerice turned to see a tri-colored swirl of black, midnight blue, and deep teal appear behind her, and she watched as the Raven Queen stepped through the portal.

Alerice looked back for Kreston, but he had vanished. She then looked about at the town folk, but was shocked to see them going about their business with no hint of alarm.

"They cannot see me," the queen said in her voice of dark honey. "You can, though. And you can see them, the innocents who needed you. This is why I sent you here. In your old life, you kept to your purpose, and I imagine it would have been another typically unremarkable life when you had finished it.

"In your new life, you have found purpose. You once claimed to be modest, but you acted in the right, and I am proud of you for doing so."

Alerice looked at her matron, but then she noticed that half a dozen ravens had begun to circle overhead. As she watched them caw and glide, she was suddenly reminded of how a similar flock had mesmerized her when riding the stolen plow horse away from Navre.

She furrowed her brow and looked into the Raven Queen's amethyst eyes. "You sent the ravens to identify me to the Reef."

"I did," the queen stated.

"But you must have known that he meant to kill me. Why did you help me die?"

"Because only through death could you begin your new life."

The queen floated forward, placed a willow-white hand on Alerice's shoulder, and guided her to turn about. Alerice watched the wagon driver climb into his seat and take up the reins to the two-horse team. Kissing to the lead, he set the wagon in motion, driving the young ones away from Basque.

"And knowing what you can now do," the queen continued, "knowing the potential of what you might yet be able to do, would you still want the life you knew before your death?"

Alerice caught sight of Honey. She had climbed out of the wagon and onto the seat next to the driver. He pulled her close, and the lassie snuggled into the crook of his arm.

"No, My Queen. I would not."

"Do you still condemn yourself?" the Raven Queen asked. "Killing Gotthard was no different from killing 'Enri. You stood up to stop the wicked. Do you still feel shame?"

Alerice took a centering breath and turned to her matron. "No, My Queen. Though I will still try to remind myself of modesty."

The Raven Queen nodded. Alerice turned back to the town and searched for Kreston, but he was nowhere to be found.

"I no longer doubt the Realme," Alerice added. "I do not doubt that I am yours to serve as you wish me to, and I am ready to live the life you have granted me."

The queen placed her willow-white hands on Alerice's armored shoulders.

"Good," she said. "You have many discoveries awaiting you, Alerice. You shall pass between worlds, between the Evherealme and Mortalia. You shall become something that I have not had in my service for many generations – a Realme Walker. All this now lies before you, my Ravensdaughter."

Tales of the Ravensdaughter
will continue with
Adventure Two
The Thief of Souls

PLEASE REVIEW THIS BOOK:

If you enjoyed ***The Beast of Basque***, please leave a review.

AMAZON

GOODREADS

AUTHOR'S WEBSITE

Thank you and blessings,
Erin Hunt Rado
ErinRadoAuthor.com

BOOKS IN THIS SERIES

Tales of the Ravensdaughter - Collection One

The Beast Of Basque

The Thief Of Souls

The Wizard And The Wyld

Rips In The Ether

Mistress Of Her Own Game

The Raven's Daughter

Made in USA - Crawfordsville, IN
31807_9798839531079
06.07.2023 1009